THE NIGHT BEFORE
CHRISTMAS

A Grosset & Dunlap **ALL ABOARD BOOK**®

Library of Congress Cataloging-in-Publication Data
Moore, Clement Clarke, 1779–1863. The night before Christmas / by Clement C. Moore ; illustrated by
Jean Hirashima. p. cm. — (All aboard books) Summary: Clement C. Moore's classic poem
describes a visit from St. Nicholas. 1. Santa Claus—Juvenile poetry. 2. Children's poetry, American.
3. Christmas—Juvenile poetry. [1. Santa Claus—Poetry. 2. Christmas—Poetry. 3. American
poetry. 4. Narrative poetry.] I. Hirashima, Jean, ill. II. Title. III. Series. PS2429.M5N5 1993
811'.2—dc20 92-27138 CIP AC ISBN 0-448-40482-6 F G H I J

Clement C. Moore

THE NIGHT BEFORE
CHRISTMAS

Illustrated by Jean Hirashima

Grosset & Dunlap, Publishers

'Twas the night before Christmas,
   when all through the house

Not a creature was stirring,
   not even a mouse;

The stockings were hung
    by the chimney with care,

In hopes that St. Nicholas
    soon would be there;

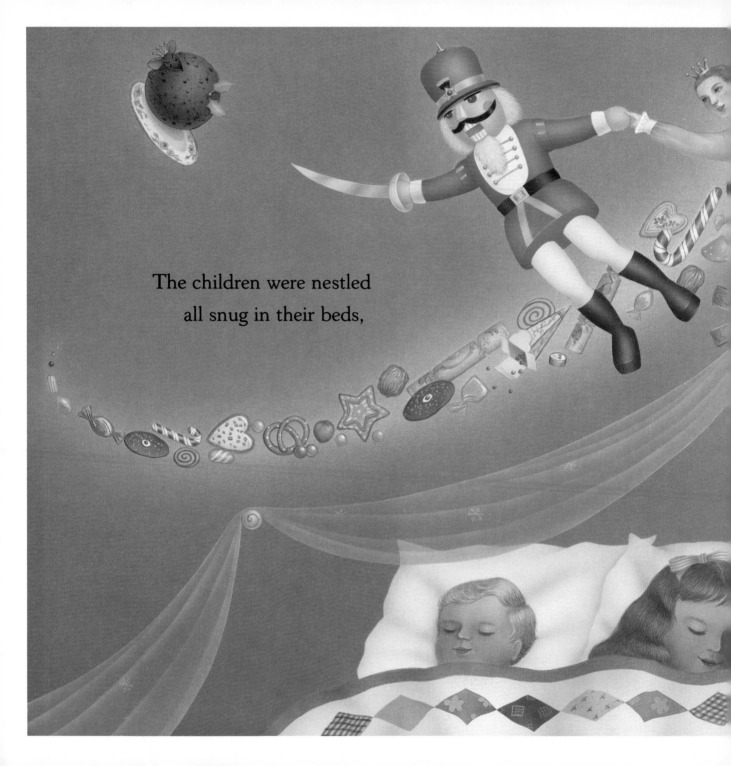

The children were nestled
all snug in their beds,

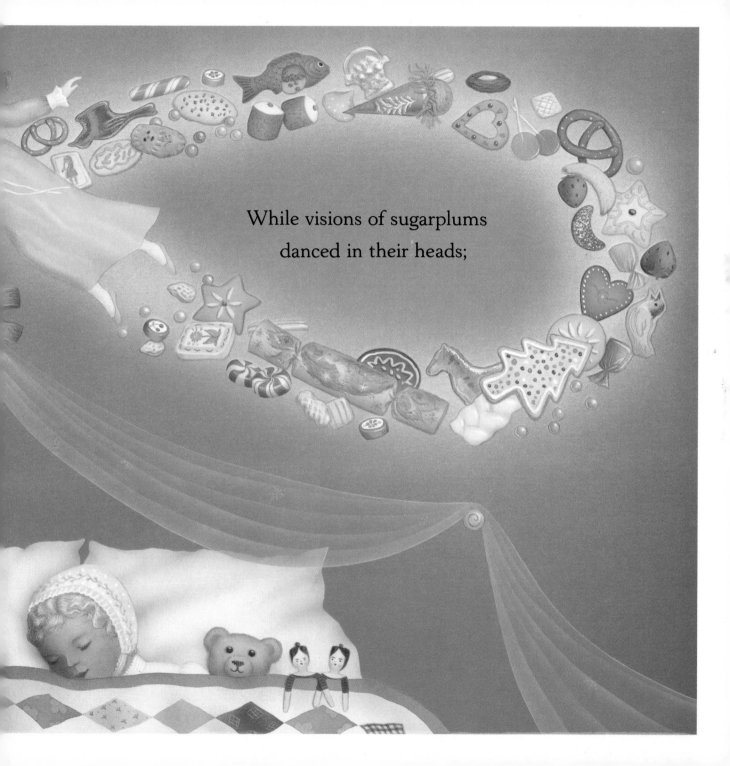

While visions of sugarplums
danced in their heads;

And Mamma in her kerchief,
and I in my cap,

Had just settled our brains
for a long winter's nap,

When out on the lawn
there arose such a clatter,

I sprang from the bed
to see what was the matter.

Away to the window
I flew like a flash,

Tore open the shutters,
and threw up the sash.

The moon on the breast
of the new-fallen snow

Gave the luster of midday
to objects below,

When, what to my wondering
eyes should appear,

But a miniature sleigh,
and eight tiny reindeer,

With a little old driver,
so lively and quick,

I knew in a moment
it must be St. Nick.

More rapid than eagles his coursers they came,
And he whistled, and shouted, and called them by name:

"Now, *Dasher*! Now, *Dancer*! Now, *Prancer* and *Vixen*!
On, *Comet*! On, *Cupid*! On, *Donder* and *Blitzen*!

To the top of the porch! To the top of the wall!
Now dash away, dash away, dash away all!"

As dry leaves that before
    the wild hurricane fly,

When they meet with an obstacle,
    mount to the sky,

So up to the housetop
    the coursers they flew,

With the sleigh full of toys,
    and St. Nicholas too.

And then, in a twinkling,
    I heard on the roof

The prancing and pawing
    of each little hoof.

As I drew in my head,
  and was turning around,

Down the chimney St. Nicholas
  came with a bound.

He was dressed all in fur,
  from his head to his foot,

And his clothes were all tarnished
  with ashes and soot;

A bundle of toys
  he had flung on his back,

And he looked like a peddler
  just opening his pack.

His eyes—how they twinkled!
  His dimples, how merry!

His cheeks were like roses,
  his nose like a cherry!

His droll little mouth
  was drawn up like a bow,

And the beard on his chin
  was as white as the snow;

The stump of a pipe
  he held tight in his teeth,

And the smoke it encircled
  his head like a wreath;

He had a broad face
    and a little round belly,

That shook, when he laughed,
    like a bowlful of jelly.

He was chubby and plump,
    a right jolly old elf,

And I laughed when I saw him,
    in spite of myself;

A wink of his eye
    and a twist of his head,

Soon gave me to know
    I had nothing to dread.

He spoke not a word,
    but went straight to his work,

And filled all the stockings;
    then turned with a jerk,

And laying his finger
    aside of his nose,

And giving a nod,
    up the chimney he rose;

He sprang to his sleigh, to his team gave a whistle,
And away they all flew like the down of a thistle.

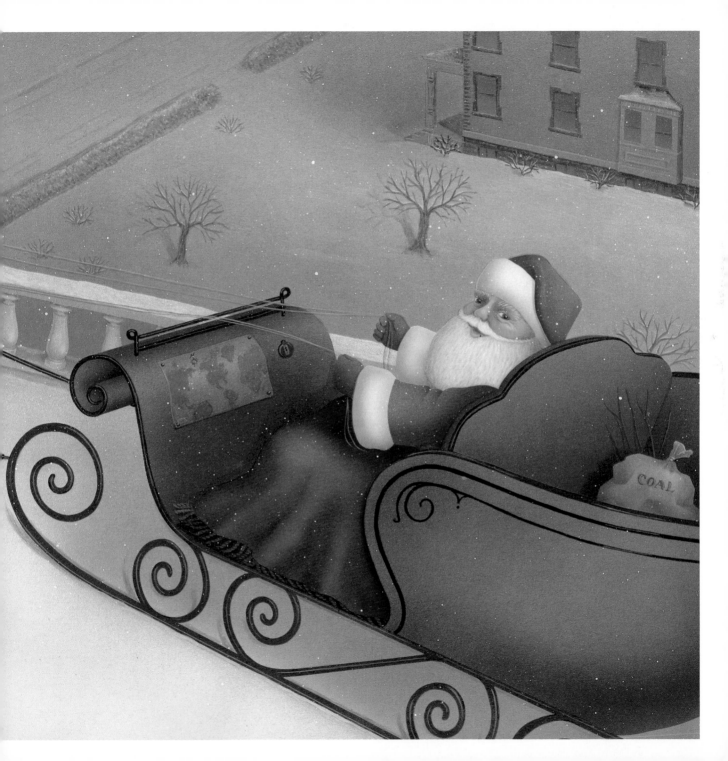

But I heard him exclaim,
　　ere he drove out of sight,

"Happy Christmas to all,
　　and to all a good-night."